W9-CDI-944

Squabbles

Written by:
Stephen Cosgrove
Illustrated by:
Robin James

A Serendipity™ Book

PRICE STERN SLOAN
Los Angeles

Dedicated to battered people everywhere and anywhere. May your wounds heal and you learn to fear no more.

Stephen

On the island of Serendipity there was a stand of trees called the Forest of Glade. Inside this clump of trees everything was always crisp and cool. Well-worn shady paths wound through the trees like gentle boulevards in a city of tall buildings. Golden leaves, tired from clinging all summer to their places in the sun, spun silently to the path below.

Things were ordered and organized here in the Forest of Glade, and even the wild flowers didn't grow wild, but were neatly planted in hanging baskets of woven wheat straw and vine.

The pristine path, bordered in flowers of quiet colors, was a meeting place of sorts for the creatures that lived in the Forest of Glade. Here, squirrel met rabbit met possum as they politely paraded their daily trade. From one end of the path to the other, they would rush hither and thither in search of this and that to make life a little easier. Along the way they would politely inquire of the weather or whether it was time to pluck the fruits from the trees.

If you looked off the path, at first seeing nothing, you would notice homes of sorts: dens, burrows and nested limbs where all the creatures lived. All was quiet here, from the muted laughter of the children playing to the wistful whispers of neighbor gossiping with neighbor.

One day in early fall there moved to the Forest of Glade a new family—a family of raccoons called the Squabbles. There was a mother and a father aptly called Momma and Poppa Squabble and a boy-child called Junior.

They appeared normal in all respects, but there was something amiss, something not quite right. For there was a wildness in the eyes of Poppa and a bit of fear if you like in the eyes of Momma and Junior.

They set up housekeeping in an old hollowed stump that sat at the edge of the path. Here the Squabbles unpacked their things, and here they felt they could always stay.

Junior scampered to the very top of the stump and looked about, nose twitching excitedly in the air. In the meantime, Momma Squabble bustled busily about her new home as Poppa pulled some weeds that somehow seemed out of place in this ordered land.

As was the custom in the Forest of Glade, a few of the creatures that had lived here for some time stopped and wished Poppa Squabble welcome. Poppa stopped his weeding task and stood with the creatures at the edge of the path and passed the time with idle chat..

From inside the stump came the gentle whines of Junior begging Momma to let him run where the other forest children ran. Momma said, "No. I'm afraid it's a little too late to be exploring." To which Junior cried, "But Momma, the other kids are still playing."

Poppa Squabble patiently ignored the ruckus at first. Then, as he tried to concentrate on his conversation, he finally said, "Excuse me for just a moment." He turned to the stump and yelled at the top of his lungs, "Be quiet in there. Our neighbors have no need of the Squabbles' squabbles." Then he turned and rejoined the conversation as if nothing at all had happened.

Of the other creatures that lived here there was a bright young bunny called Buttermilk who became Junior's best friend. The two of them would scamper about playing nose tag or hide-and-go-sneak. For days and days they had played together just like all other creatures in the forest.

But one morning Junior was late for play, and when he came his tail was dragging and a tear refused to dry in his eye. Buttermilk rushed to her friend and hurriedly asked, "What happened? Why are you late, and why do you cry?"

Junior brushed the tear from his eye and sullenly said, "Nothing's the matter. I'm late because. . . I, uh. . . fell out of bed. And I'm crying because it hurts."

Sure enough, Buttermilk could see welts and bruises all over the little raccoon's cheek and arms that could have happened if someone fell hard from bed.

They frolicked and played the rest of the day, as a raccoon and bunny were wont to do in field and forest alike. Later they even played a game at Junior's house. It was late afternoon when their play was interrupted by Momma Squabble. "Buttermilk," she asked, "would you care for some cookies and milk?"

"Yes, thank you," answered Buttermilk politely. She grinned at Junior who made a face at her as they waited for their afternoon treat. As the mother raccoon bustled about, Buttermilk noticed that Momma Squabble had bruises and bumps on her cheeks and arms, too, and her eye was as black as a boot heel. "Gee whiz, Mizz Squabble," gushed Buttermilk. "Did you fall out of bed, too?"

Momma Squabble shot a curious look at Junior, who stared into his glass of milk. "Yes, yes, Buttermilk," she flustered as she nervously touched hand to cheek. "I fell out of bed, too."

Buttermilk didn't think anything more about it until later that night as the stars exploded in the purple crystal sky. She was rushing home, having just run an errand, when she heard shouting noises coming from the stump where the Squabbles lived. She stopped for a moment, afraid to move and afraid not to.

For the voice that was yelling was none other than Poppa Squabble himself. He shouted that everything was wrong, from Momma's dinner to Junior's chores. His bellowing was softened only by the gentle consoling of Momma Squabble as she urged him, begged him, not to get mad.

"Don't get mad?" he shouted. "You are telling me not to get mad?" Softer now, and yet even more threatening, Poppa Squabble continued, "I'm not going to get mad. . . I am going to get the belt."

Through the open window Buttermilk could see him storm from the room. Her stomach was aching and she didn't know why. Tears welled in her eyes as she watched her friend and his mother cower in their own home. Buttermilk could watch no more. She rushed home as a single stifled cry echoed into the stillness of the night.

The little rabbit burst into the house and into her father's arms. "My, my," he said. "Why the tears, my little Buttermilk Bunny?"

"Oh, daddy," she cried. "I just saw and heard the most horrible things and I don't know what to do."

Her father picked her up and said, "There is nothing so horrible seen nor heard that you can't tell me or your mother."

With that Buttermilk told him of the bumps and bruises she had seen that morning and all that she had seen outside the stump.

Leaving Buttermilk at home, her father rushed down the path to where the Squabbles lived. There he was joined by others of the glade who had heard all the goings on. Sure enough, inside the stump through the window opened wide was Poppa Squabble threatening Momma and Junior with a belt.

All the creatures on the path quickly huddled together. "What should we do?" they asked one another. "Should we rush in and stop this beating?"

"It is spoken," said one, "that all creatures have a right to privacy in their own home."

"Yes," whispered Buttermilk's father through clenched teeth, "but not when they are beating those smaller than themselves. No one has that right."

They all rushed to the door and with great furry fists they rapped. The yelling stopped inside and all was quiet. Slowly the door opened and there stood Poppa Squabble, the belt still held in his hand, "What do you want?" he asked gruffly.

"We want," said Buttermilk's father coolly, "for you to stop beating your wife and child."

"Harrumph," puffed Poppa Squabble. "They are mine and I will do with them as I please." With that he began to close the door.

"No," said the rabbit. "They are not yours to own and do with as you please. For they have rights, too." Boldly he reached out and grabbed Poppa Squabble firmly by the arm and led him from the stump as the others consoled the mother and her child.

By the next day things had settled down in the Glade, but few had forgotten nor ever would. Oddly enough, Poppa Squabble really loved his family, but just couldn't control his anger.

For a while he lived apart from his family, and in that time he learned those lessons that must be learned. He learned that a family is not a possession. He learned not to strike others in anger. But most of all, he learned that forgiveness can be earned only by deed.

AS YOU LOOK AROUND AT FRIENDS
WHETHER BUNNY, SQUIRREL OR OTHER
REACH OUT A HELPING HAND
FOR WE ARE EACH OTHER'S BROTHERS

Serendipity™ Books

Written by Stephen Cosgrove
Illustrated by Robin James

Enjoy all the delightful books in the Serendipity Series:

The above books, and many others, can be bought wherever books are sold, or may be ordered directly from the publisher.

PRICE STERN SLOAN
360 North La Cienega Boulevard, Los Angeles, California 90048